The Signalman &
Holiday Romance

The Signalman & Holiday Romance

Level 600 Reader (L+) (CEFR B1-B2)

Charles J. H. Dickens

Josh MacKinnon (Adaptor)
John McLean (Series Editor)

MATATABI PRESS

Charles J. H. Dickens (1858)
Photograph by George Herbert Watkins

Charles John Huffman Dickens was born in 1812 in the city of Portsmouth, England. He loved to read and learn from an early age. However, when he was twelve, his family ran into money troubles and his father went to jail for not paying his debts. This forced Charles to leave school and start working to help out. Even though his schooling stopped early, Dickens didn't let this hold him back. He grew up to be a famous British writer, creating fifteen novels, five short novels, and many short stories. His story *A Christmas Carol* from 1843 is still much-loved today. It's been turned into plays, movies, and cartoons that families all over the world watch at Christmas.

In 1866, Dickens wrote *The Signalman*, featuring an unnamed narrator encountering a railway signalman who shares his spooky experiences, such as seeing a ghostly figure of a man and witnessing unusual events on the railway line. The tale, known for its haunting and atmospheric qualities, is often referred to as a classic of the ghost story genre.

Two years later, in 1868, Dickens authored *Holiday Romance*, released in installments in a children's magazine. This work differed from many of his other novels, offering lighthearted tales from a child's perspective. Unlike his usual focus on societal issues seen through children's eyes, *Holiday Romance* aimed at lighthearted adventures and fostering imaginative play.

Dickens died in 1870 when he was 58 years old. He

was buried in Westminster Abbey in London, a special place where many great writers are remembered.

First Printing: July 2021 — *Holiday Romance: Level 600 Reader (J)*
Second Printing: February 2024 — *The Signalman & Holiday Roman:
Level 600 Reader (L+) (CEFR B1-B2)*

MATATABI PRESS (910554)
Windwhistle, Farley Hill, Matlock. DE4 3LL. UK
20-20, 5-Chome, Yamamoto-shinmachi, Asaminami-ku, Hiroshima.
731-0139. JAPAN
https://www.press.matatabi-japan.com/
https://www.holdings.matatabi-japan.com/
Email: press@matatabi-japan.com
Tel: 0081-(0)70-8592-2501

Special thanks are owed to the students from the Department of English at Yasuda Women's University in Hiroshima, Japan. During the final editing stages, they conscientiously checked and tested the stories in this book to enhance its suitability for EFL and ESL students globally.

CONTENTS

THE SIGNALMAN

HOLIDAY ROMANCE

CONTENTS

THE SIGNALMAN

1.1 The Mysterious Signalman

As I looked down at the railway tracks, I saw a signalman standing in front of the signal-box, with a flag neatly tucked under his arm. "Hello, below!"

I called out. However, instead of looking up at me, he stared along the tracks into a tunnel. 'That's strange,' I thought to myself.

"Hello, below!" I called again. This time, he noticed me. "May I come down to talk to you?" I asked.

He didn't reply, so I stood waiting patiently. Then suddenly, the ground and air shook—a train was coming. The loud noise surprised me. After it had passed, the signalman looked up at me again.

"May I come down to talk to you?" I asked once more. He looked at me thoughtfully for a moment before pointing toward a path that led down to the track. "All right!" I said, and I headed toward the steep path. It zigzagged down to the tracks.

After reaching the tracks, I walked slowly toward him. As I got closer, I noticed his dark beard and heavy eyebrows. His look was fixed; he seemed lost in thought. His workplace was very lonely and sad. The area was wet. There was hardly any sunlight. It smelled strange, and cold winds blew along the tracks.

He stayed completely still until I stopped right in front of him. Then, he stepped back a bit.

"It seems very lonely working here," I commented. "I noticed this place from above," I continued, trying to start a light conversation. "I guess not many people come this way. I hope it's okay that I came down for a chat." I'm not great at starting conversations, and something about the signalman made me feel uneasy.

He turned away from me and looked towards the red light at the tunnel entrance, checking it as if he thought something was wrong. Then, he looked at me again.

"Is that light part of your job?" I asked him, hoping to break the silence.

He spoke softly, "Yes, it is."

I looked into his serious eyes and firm face. Suddenly, I thought he might not be real, maybe he was a ghost, or maybe my visiting him was making him unhappy.

I moved back a little. Then, I saw a little bit of fear in his eyes. This made me stop thinking he was a ghost.

"Did I say or do something that made you feel scared?" I asked, smiling.

"I wasn't sure if I'd seen you before," he answered.

"Where?" I wanted to know.

He pointed toward the red light at the entrance to the tunnel.

"Over there?" I asked.

He didn't say anything but nodded his head.

"I have never been over there," I told him.

"Thank you," he replied, relaxing a little.

His mood got better and so did mine. He was happy to answer my questions. "Do you have a lot of work here?" I asked.

"Yes," he said, "I have to be very careful and do things just right."

He told me that he was used to working long hours alone. He had even used his time alone to learn a new language, but he could only read it and guessed at how to speak it. He had tried to learn some mathematics too, like fractions, decimals, and a little algebra, but admitted he was never good with numbers, even when he was young.

"Do you always have to stay in this dark and wet place?" I asked. "Don't you ever get to go outside?" He told me that he sometimes got out into the sunlight for a short time, but he had to stay close enough to the signal-box to hear the bell ring.

He took me into his office in the signal-box. There was a small fire burning, a desk, a machine for sending messages, and the bell. When I tried to compliment him on his learning, he didn't make a big deal of it. He told me it's common for us all to end up working in places we might not expect. He used to study science when he was younger and went to classes, but he said he didn't use his chances well and now it was too late to change his life path. He knew that he had made mistakes and accepted that this was his job now.

He talked in a steady voice, sometimes calling me "Sir," especially when he talked about his younger days. It seemed like he wanted to show me that he was just an ordinary person. He often had to stop talking to listen for his bell, and he had other work too, like showing flags to trains and talking to the drivers. He was careful with his work, but I saw him look pale and check the bell twice, even though it didn't ring. He also sometimes opened the door to check the red light near the tunnel. After looking, he would come back to sit by the fire and seemed to have something on his mind. This made me a bit worried, even though he was just doing his job well.

When it was time for me to go, I tried to keep the conversation going and said, "It seems like you're a happy man."

"I think I was once," he answered, speaking softly as he had before. "However, something is bothering me now, Sir."

He seemed like he wished he hadn't said that, but I asked him anyway, "What's wrong? What's on your mind?"

"It's hard to explain, Sir. If you come to see me again, I'll tell you more."

"I do want to come back," I said. "When should I visit?"

"I'll be here at ten o'clock tomorrow night, Sir," he replied.

"Okay, I'll come here at eleven."

He thanked me and walked with me. "I'll keep my light on until you find the way up. Once you find it, don't call out! And when you come back down tomorrow night, don't call out either! Let me ask you one last thing. Why did you call out 'Hello, below!' tonight?"

"I don't know," I replied. "I guess I said something like that—"

"Not something like that, Sir. Those were your exact words," he said.

"Okay, they were the exact words. I said them because I was up there and I saw you below."

"Did you feel like the words came to you in a mysterious way?"

"No."

He said goodbye and lifted his light. I walked alongside the railway tracks, feeling worried about a train coming from behind, until I found the path. It was easier going up than coming down.

Quiz 1.1

1. Why did the narrator call out to the signalman?
2. How did the signalman initially react to the narrator's call?
3. Describe the setting where the signalman worked.
4. What tasks did the signalman need to perform?
5. What did the signalman share about his background and education?
6. How did the signalman seem to feel during the conversation with the narrator?
7. How did the signalman suggest the narrator to return for another visit?

1.2 Visions and Warning Signals

As planned, the next night at eleven, I began to walk down the steep path. The signalman was waiting for me at the bottom with his light on. "I didn't call out," I told him as we met. "Can I talk now?"

"Of course, Sir."

"Okay then, good evening." I shook his hand.

"Good evening, Sir." We then went together to his office, went inside, closed the door, and sat down by the fire.

"I have decided, Sir," he started in a quiet voice, "that I will tell you what's bothering me. Yesterday, I mistook you for someone else who is causing trouble for me."

"Who is it?" I asked.

"I don't know."

"Does he look like me?"

"I don't know," he said. "I never saw his face. He covered it with his left arm and waved at me with his right."

The signalman then described a night when the moon was shining brightly. He had heard someone shouting, "Hello, below!" so he ran to the door and saw someone near the red light at the tunnel, waving. The voice was rough and kept yelling, "Look out!" The signalman changed the light to red and hurried to the man, asking, "What's wrong?" However, when he got close to the dark tunnel, the man disappeared.

I asked if the man had gone into the tunnel. "No, he did not," the signalman replied. "I went down the tunnel for a long distance, then came back and checked the area near to the red light, but no one was there."

"Maybe it was your imagination," I suggested, pointing out the strange sounds around, like the wind and the telephone wires.

He continued with his story explaining that six hours after seeing the man, there was a bad accident on the railway tracks. Then, a few hours after that, the victims were carried out of the tunnel, right where he had seen the man standing. He placed his hand on my arm and looked back over his shoulder. "All of this happened exactly one year ago," he said. "Then, a few months ago, I saw the man again. He was standing by the red light." He paused and stared at me.

"Did the man say anything?" I asked.

"No, he was quiet."

"Did he wave at you?"

"No, he just leaned against the light post, covering his face with both hands. Like this."

"Did you approach him?"

"No, I came back into my office. I wanted to sit down and calmly think about what I had seen. When I looked out of the door again, it was daylight and the man was gone."

"Was there another accident after that?" I asked.

He nodded sadly. "Later that day, as a train came out of the tunnel, I saw a lot of movement at a window on my side of a train. Someone was waving. I signaled to the driver to stop. I heard terrible screams and cries from inside of the train.

A young woman had died instantly in one of the compartments. The other passengers brought her in here and laid on the floor."

I couldn't find any words to say. My mouth was very dry.

He continued. "Now, Sir, listen to this and see how troubled I am. The man came back a week ago."

"At the red light?"

"Yes, at the red light," the signalman said. "This time, he called out to me for many minutes in a pained way, 'Hello, below! Look out! Look out!' He kept waving at me and making my bell ring—"

I interrupted. "Did the man ring your bell yesterday when I was here?"

"Yes, twice."

"Your mind is playing tricks on you," I said. "I was watching and listening to the bell, and it didn't ring those two times when you went out to look."

He shook his head. "I've never made a mistake about that, Sir. I've never mixed up that ghostly man's ring with a real one. The man's ring is different. The bell vibrates and the bell moves visibly. I understand why you didn't hear it, but I did."

"And was the ghostly man there when you looked out?" I asked

"Yes, he WAS there."

"Both times?"

He firmly repeated: "Yes, both times."

I stood up and walked toward the door. "Join me," I suggested. "Let's see if he is there now."

He looked hesitant but finally got up and joined me at the door. I opened it and stood on the step while he stood in the doorway. I could see the red light, the dark tunnel mouth, the tall, damp stone walls, and the stars above them.

"Do you see the man?" I asked him, carefully observing his face.

"No," he replied. "He's not there."

"Agreed," I said.

We went back into his office, closed the door, and sat down again. He started speaking, "By now, you'll understand, Sir," he said, "that what troubles me so much is this question: What does he want to warn me about this time? Where is the danger? Will another terrible disaster happen?" He wiped the sweat from his heated forehead with his hand-kerchief. "If I send a warning of danger to the train drivers," he continued, "I have no explanation for it. I'd get in trouble. They'd think I was insane."

His pain was truly distressing to see. It was the torment of a responsible man, overwhelmed by a duty tied to protecting lives.

The signalman continued, clearly distressed. He wished that the ghostly man had given him information that is more specific. "Why is the message simply that someone is going to die?" he complained.

I tried to calm him, remaining with him until 2 a.m. I offered to stay through the night, but he declined. Before leaving, I agreed to return the following night. As I walked back, I couldn't help but feel uneasy and on edge about the sighting of the ghostly man and the accidents. I also worried about the signalman's mental health and his ability to do his job reliably.

Quiz 1.2

1. When did the narrator come back to talk to the signalman the next night?
2. How did the signalman react and behave when the narrator met him at the bottom of the steep path?
3. What did the signalman say about the person he mistook the narrator for?
4. Can you explain what happened when someone was seen waving near the red light in the tunnel, as mentioned by the signalman?
5. What worried the signalman and why did he feel troubled when encountering the mysterious man?
6. What did the narrator notice about the bell ringing by the ghostly man and the actual bell ringing?
7. Why was the signalman concerned about cautioning the train drivers about danger, and why did he find it a difficult situation?

1.3 A Chilling Revelation

The next evening, I decided to encourage the signalman to see a doctor. As I approached the train tracks, I looked down from the same place as before, and, to my surprise, I saw a man standing next to the red light. He was covering his face with his left arm and waving his right arm. There were other men around him. He was certainly a man and not a ghost. Feeling a deep sense that something was wrong, I went down the steep path as fast as I could and asked the men what had happened.

"The signalman was killed this morning, Sir," one of them said.

"The man from that signal-box?" I inquired

"Yes, Sir."

"How did it happen?"

"He was hit by a train, Sir. The train came out of the tunnel and hit him. Tom, please tell the gentleman what happened."

Tom, the train driver, walked toward the tunnel entrance and pointed in. "As I turned the corner in the tunnel, Sir," he said, "I saw the signalman at the end. I didn't have time to slow down. I turned off the engine and shouted as loudly as I could."

"What did you say?" I asked.

"Hello, below! Look out! Look out!"

I was stunned.

"Ah, it was a terrible moment, Sir. I covered my eyes with my left arm, like this, and waved my right arm, like this, but it was no use."

I want to highlight something without emphasizing one detail over the others. The warning called out by the train driver included not just the words that the signalman had said troubled him, but also the words that I, not the signalman, had connected in my mind to the actions he had copied.

Quiz 1.3

1. What choice did the narrator make about the signalman the next evening?
2. Can you describe what the narrator saw when coming closer to the train tracks?
3. What happened to the signalman according to one of the men the narrator met?
4. How did the train driver, Tom, explain what happened that led to the signalman's death?
5. What did the train driver shout as he neared the signalman at the tunnel's end?
6. What detail did the narrator find important in the train driver's warning, connecting it to the signalman's past?
7. How did the train driver try to warn the signalman about the danger, and what sadly happened despite his attempts?

HOLIDAY ROMANCE

2.1 William (Aged 8)

Hello, I'm William, and I oversaw the writing of the following four stories. The first story, below, is entirely true, and it's essential that you believe everything in it.

Nettie is my wife. We first met at dance school. I used my own money to buy her a green ring from a toyshop. We got married in the dance school closet. Robin, my cousin, and Alice were present as witnesses. After the wedding, we went for a walk along the country road. Robin lit a firework to celebrate our marriage.

The next day, Robin and Alice also had a similar wedding, where a firework made a loud noise that startled a nearby dog.

Nettie, my wife, and Alice, Robin's wife, were held captive at Ms. Grimmer's house. Ms. Grimmer lived there with her mean partner, Ms. Drowvey. At first, Robin and I planned to rescue Nettie and Alice the next Wednesday using fireworks. However, because fireworks in the nearby shop were so expensive, we had to change our plan.

On Wednesday, Robin showed up at my house at 2 p.m. with a black flag and a small knife. He had a plan written on a piece of paper. It showed me behind a streetlight, with big ears, which I don't have. According to Robin's plan, I was to wait behind the streetlight until he knocked Drowvey to the ground. Then, I was to get my wife, Nettie, and run together to the country road. If needed, I had to fight anybody who tried to stop us.

Robin and I positioned ourselves near Drowvey's house, waiting for the right moment. After a while, Drowvey, Grimmer, Nettie, and Alice came out. Robin started the attack, but it wasn't successful. Drowvey and Grimmer fought back. I followed our plan, waiting for Robin to knock down Drowvey. When that didn't happen, I continued to the next phase of our plan. I ran toward the country road, prepared to attack anybody who got in my way. Luckily, no one did.

I waited and waited for Robin. When he finally arrived at the country road, he said that our plan had failed because Drowvey was too stubborn to fall to the ground.

The next day at dance school, my wife, Nettie, gave me a note without saying a word. I opened the note: "Is my husband a cow?"

A cow? Why would she call me a cow? What does it mean? After the dance, I showed the note to Robin.

"She missed the 'a-r-d' from the end of 'cow,'" he explained.

"Cow, a-r-d?" I said loudly.

"Cow—cow—coward," he whispered. "She thinks you were too scared to attack Drowvey and Grimmer."

I strongly denied being a coward and asked Robin to arrange a trial in court to prove I wasn't. He agreed.

Arranging a trial was quite difficult. For example, Napoleon, the Emperor of France, had difficulty leaving his house due to his aunt. He had to climb over the back wall of his garden to get out.

The trial took place by the pond on the grass under a weeping willow tree. My personal enemy, Richard, was present. I was taken into the court by two guards, and Nettie sat under an umbrella. James B., who we considered to be the President of the United States of America, stood up and asked, "Coward or no coward, guilty or not guilty?"

I firmly answered, "Not a coward and not guilty." Richard then questioned Alice and Nettie about my behavior.

Later, Robin came into the court holding a piece of paper, something I had been waiting for. I broke free from the guards and asked Robin to tell everyone the most important part during an attack. However, before he could answer, Richard interrupted, saying, "Courage."

Richard's rude comment made the President of the United States of America very angry. He told the guards to put leaves into Richard's mouth. Then, I turned to Robin and asked him what the most important thing during an attack is. "Is it following orders?" I said.

"Yes, it is," he firmly replied.

I asked if the paper he had was the plan to free Nettie and Alice. It was. When everyone in the court learned that I had followed my orders, they cheered loudly. Unfortunately, before the President could say that I wasn't a coward and was not guilty, Napoleon's aunt dragged him from the court, and the trial ended before judgement could be passed.

The following evening, under the moonlight, Robin, Alice, Nettie, and I met again at the court. We sat under the willow tree. Nettie and Alice looked quietly at the pond. Minutes passed without anybody talking. Then, Alice said, "We have to stop pretending. We have to give it up."

"Ha!" said Robin. "Pretending?"

"Please, Robin. You worry me," said Alice.

My wife, Nettie, felt the same way. Robin and I looked at each other without speaking.

"If adults won't act responsibly and continue to punish us, why should we keep pretending?" said Alice.

"We just end up in trouble," Nettie added.

"Robin, you know," continued Alice, "Drowvey didn't fall to the ground, and the trial ended badly. Now think about our marriage. Do you really think my family will accept it?"

"Do you really think my family will accept our marriage, William?" Nettie asked.

Robin and I looked at each other again.

"Robin, if you came to my house and tried to claim me as your wife, you'd get in trouble," Alice explained.

"And William, if you did the same at my family's house, you'd have things thrown at you from the window," Nettie said.

Robin stood up. "I would refuse to leave your house without you!" he shouted.

"What if the adults fight back?" asked Alice.

"Then, I will keep fighting them until they let me take you," Robin said.

"What if they don't?" Alice replied.

"Are your feelings still strong for me, Alice?" asked Robin.

"Robin! I will always love you," said Alice.

"Are your feelings still strong for me, Nettie?" I inquired.

"William! I will be yours for all time," replied Nettie.

All four of us hugged. Do not misunderstand; Robin hugged Alice, and I hugged Nettie. However, two and two make four.

"Nettie and I have thought carefully," said Alice. "The adults have too much control over us. They make fun of us and have changed our world. William, your younger brother had a naming ceremony yesterday. Did a king attend the ceremony?"

"No," I replied.

"Any queens?" Nettie inquired.

"No queens were present. Perhaps one was present in the kitchen, but no one mentioned it," I said.

"Any fairies?"

"None to be seen."

"Did Grimmer attend the ceremony pretending to be a mean witch and give your baby brother a bad gift?" asked Alice. "Answer, William."

Mother did say that Uncle Chopper's gift was not so good, but she didn't say it was bad.

"The adults have changed our world," said Alice.

"They are bad people!" protested Robin.

"No, Robin, Darling," said Alice, "don't say that. It does not help."

"There is only one solution," said Alice. "We must guide the adults so that they can understand us better. We must pretend in a different way. We must wait calmly."

"How?" Robin asked, looking unhappy. Four and a half teeth were missing from the front of his mouth. Half of one tooth remained because he had escaped during his last visit to the dentist. "How can we guide them? How can we pretend in a different way? How can we wait?" demanded Robin.

"This is our last night together, isn't it, Robin?" said Alice. "Let's take this time to think about how we can guide the adults. Let us come up with a plan to tell them the right way to behave. William, you are the best writer, so you should write down our thoughts. Is that okay with everyone?"

"I suppose so," agreed Robin, "but how can we pretend in a different way?"

"Robin, we will keep pretending," said Alice. "We will act like children, but stop pretending to be those adults who can't understand us."

Robin was sad. "How long do I have to wait?" he complained.

Alice held Nettie's hand and looked up. "We will stay strong until a change happens. We will wait until adults stop making fun of us. We will keep waiting until the fairies return. If needed, we will wait until we are 80, 90, or even older. Then, the fairies will send us children, and we will help these children a lot."

"We will, Alice," agreed Nettie, hugging her. "Now, William, go and get some cherries for us. I will give you the money."

I asked Robin to come with me, but he was too upset. He had started pulling up grass and chewing on it. When I returned with the cherries, though,

Alice had calmed him down. She told him that we would all soon reach the age of 90.

Sitting under the willow tree and eating the cherries, we pretended to be 90 years old. Nettie complained of an ache in her old back, while Alice sang like an old woman. Alice said she needed new slippers. She mentioned feeling very old and having achy knees, and I felt the same. It was lovely. We were all happy.

There were too many cherries to eat, so Alice and Nettie made cherry-wine to celebrate our time together. Each of us drank from a small wineglass that was hidden in Alice's bag. It was delicious. When it was Alice's turn to drink from the glass, she raised it up and said, "To our friendship." Robin drank his wine last, tears shining in his eyes.

A few minutes later, looking around, I saw nothing but the moonlit atmosphere under the willow tree. Nettie and Alice were gone. Tears rolled down my face.

Robin and I stayed under the willow tree for some time, embarrassed about our red, teary eyes. That evening, during dinner, everyone noticed that

I was walking like an old man, and I was proud that they recognized this.

Quiz 2.1

1. Who is in charge of writing the four stories?
2. How did William and Nettie first meet?
3. Why did Robin light a firework after William's wedding?
4. What was the initial plan to rescue Nettie and Alice from Ms. Grimmer's house?
5. What did Nettie's note to William imply when she called him a "cow"?
6. What was the outcome of the trial that was arranged to prove William wasn't a coward?
7. How did the group pretend to be older while sharing cherries under the willow tree?

2.2 Nettie (Aged 6.5)

There's a country where the children control everything. It's a wonderful country. In this country, grown-ups are called adult-children, and when they are very old, we call them adult-babies. They must do everything the children say. They must go to bed early and can only have snacks at night on their birthdays. The children tell them to make jam, jelly, cakes, pies and desserts. If the adult-children don't do as they're told, they're made to sit in a corner of the room. However, if they are good, they're sometimes given dessert.

Ms. Orange lived in this nice country. She was a kind girl, but her parents did not behave well. Her parents' friends made trouble too. One day, Ms. Orange said to herself, "These adult-children are too troublesome. I'm going to send them all to school."

Ms. Orange put on a pretty dress and carried her heavy adult-baby. She went to Ms. Lemon's house. Ms. Lemon was the head of a school for adult-children. Ms. Orange rang the bell. The cleaner opened the door. "Good morning," said Ms. Orange. "It's nice weather today, isn't it? Can I talk to Ms. Lemon?"

"Yes, Madam."

"Please tell her Nettie Orange is here with her adult-baby."

"Yes. Come in and wait in the living room."

Ms. Lemon came into the living room with her heavy adult-baby. "Good morning, Ms. Lemon. It's a nice day, isn't it? How are you and your adult-baby?" Ms. Orange asked.

"Thank you for asking," Ms. Lemon replied. "I'm fine, but my adult-baby is a little sick. I think her teeth are hurting."

"Oh, I see," said Ms. Orange. "I hope she doesn't cry too much. How many teeth does she have?"

"Five," said Ms. Lemon, looking at her adult-baby's mouth.

"My adult-baby has eight teeth," said Ms. Orange. "Let's put them down on the rug while we talk."

"Yes, let's do that," said Ms. Lemon. "They're so heavy."

Changing the subject, Ms. Orange asked, "Ms. Lemon, I want to know if your school has room for more adult-children."

"Yes. How many do you require?"

"Well, Ms. Lemon, all eight of my adult-children are becoming too hard to control. I look after two parents, two of their close friends, one uncle, and three aunts. Do you have vacancies for eight adult-children?"

"I have exactly eight vacancies," said Ms. Lemon.

"That's great! Does it cost a lot of money?"

"No, the fees are very reasonable, Ms. Orange."

"Is the food good?"

"Yes, it's excellent," said Ms. Lemon.

"Do you hit the adult-children when they're bad?" asked Ms. Orange.

"Sometimes we gently tap them if they do something very bad," said Ms. Lemon.

"Thank you. Can you show me around the school, Ms. Lemon?"

"Of course. Follow me, Ms. Orange."

Ms. Lemon took Ms. Orange into the schoolroom. "Get up, Adult-children," said Ms. Lemon. All of the adult-children stood up.

"Why is the man with the red beard in the corner? Did he do something bad?" asked Ms. Orange.

Ms. Lemon called the adult-boy over. "Come here, Mr. White. Tell this lady why I made you stand in the corner of the room."

"I've been gambling, Madam," said Mr. White.

"Are you sorry for what you did?" asked Ms. Lemon.

"No, I'm not," he yelled. "I only feel sorry if I lose money."

"He's a bad one," said Ms. Lemon. "Return to the corner, Mr. White, and stay there until you're ready to apologize."

Ms. Lemon pointed to another adult-boy. "That's Mr. Brown. He has a very serious problem.

He eats and drinks too much. He's greedy. How are your knees today, Mr. Brown?"

"Very painful," replied Mr. Brown.

"Well, it's because you're overweight, Mr. Brown," said Ms. Lemon. "Your stomach is the size of two stomachs. Go and exercise right now."

Next, Ms. Lemon pointed to an adult-girl. "That's Ms. Black. She's always running around, getting her clothes dirty. Come here, Ms. Black. Well, Ms. Black, are you going to improve your behavior?"

"I don't want to improve my behavior," yelled Ms. Black. "I just don't want to!"

"She won't take advice from anybody, and she gets angry so quickly," said Ms. Lemon. "If you watch her running around laughing, you might think she's cheerful and friendly. However, she's as bad as the worst of them!"

"Looking after all of these troublesome adult-children must be such hard work," said Ms. Orange.

"It is. It is," said Ms. Lemon. "They always shout and complain. They fight all day. They are mean and think they are better than others."

"Thank you, Ms. Lemon. It was very kind of you to show me around your school. I'll go home now and get my adult-children ready to come here," said Ms. Orange.

"It was my pleasure, Ms. Orange. I'll make sure that their beds are ready when they arrive," said Ms. Lemon.

Ms. Orange picked up her adult-baby and went home. As soon as she arrived at the house, she told her adult-children to pack their bags. They refused, of course, but it was no good. Ms. Orange took them to the school, wished them good luck, and waved goodbye.

"How wonderful! I can finally take a rest!" said Ms. Orange, sitting down on her armchair.

Just then, Ms. Ali rang Ms. Orange's doorbell.

"Ms. Ali," said Ms. Orange, "it's nice to see you. Come in, please. I'm about to eat lunch. Join me. I'm having some sweet stuff followed by a dish of sweet bread and sweet dessert?"

"Thank you so much, Ms. Orange. Actually, I came to invite you to a party," said Ms. Ali.

"A party?" repeated Ms. Orange.

"Yes, we're having a small party at our house

tonight for all of the adult-children in the neighborhood. I hope that you, Mr. Orange, and your adult-baby can join us."

"Yes! We'd love to!" said Ms. Orange.

"Excellent!" said Ms. Ali.

Just then, Mr. Orange came home from the city.

"William, Darling," said Ms. Orange, "you look tired. Did you have a busy day in the city?"

"Yes, I was pushing and pulling tables all day long, Nettie," said Mr. Orange. "It was such hard work."

"What a terrible place to work, William," said Ms. Orange, gently pressing his arm.

Lunch was ready. They sat down to eat. Mr. Orange cut the sweet stuff into slices. "Let's celebrate," he said. "Nettie, Darling, bring a bottle of our best ginger-beer."

In the evening, Mr. and Ms. Orange, and their adult-baby went to Ms. Ali's house. Ms. Ali had decorated her room with lots of paper flowers.

"How beautiful!" said Ms. Orange. "The adult-children will be happy."

Mr. Orange looked at the decorations. "I'm not

really interested in adult-children," he said, shaking his head.

"Surely, you like adult-girls," said Ms. Ali.

Mr. Orange shook his head. "They all think that they are more important than everybody else."

"William, Darling, look at this," said Ms. Orange "Isn't it wonderful! Ms. Ali has prepared dinner for the adult-children. Here's their little salmon! Here's their little salad, their little roast beef, and their tiny, tiny, tiny glasses of champagne!"

"I think it's best if the adult-children have dinner in the back room by themselves," said Ms. Ali. "Our table is in the corner over here."

The adult-children started to arrive. The first was an overweight adult-boy. He was wearing glasses. The housecleaner brought him in. "Hello, come in," said Ms. Ali. "Sit down at that table. You will get a drink soon."

Next, more adult-children arrived. Some of them started to behave badly as soon as they entered the house. They were walking around with cups of tea or coffee in their hands. Four very fat and very boring adult-boys were standing in the doorway, talking about newspapers. Ms. Ali scolded them.

"Boys, no one can get in or out of the house if you stand there. Move or I will send you home." One adult-boy with a beard was standing on the rug in front of the fire. He was warming his back. Ms. Ali sent him home first. "Your behavior is very bad," she said, pushing him out of the house.

A band started to play music. One adult-child played the harp. One played the cornet, and one, the piano. Ms. Ali and Ms. Orange told the adult-children to find a dance partner. Many of the adult-boys refused to dance. Some of them politely said, "Not now, maybe later," while others loudly yelled, "I never dance!"

"These adult-children are so stubborn! Looking after them is such hard work," said Ms. Ali to Ms. Orange.

"I agree. They're lovely, but they really are troublesome," said Ms. Orange to Ms. Ali.

After some time, the adult-children became a little quieter. Some of the adult-boys started to slide around the dance floor. However, they still refused to dance.

The adult-boys were so troublesome. First, they refused to dance. Then, all of a sudden, they would start to dance and sing by themselves. "If you continue to behave badly," said Ms. Ali to a tall adult-boy, "I'll send you to bed immediately."

The adult-girls were wearing very long dresses. In fact, they were so long that they dragged along the floor. The adult-boys kept accidently standing on the dresses. Whenever this happened, the adult-girls angrily yelled, screamed and shook their fists.

One thing that made everybody happy was when Ms. Ali yelled, "Dinner is ready!" All of the adult-children ran to the table, pushing and yelling at one another.

"How are the adult-children getting on, Darling?" Mr. Orange asked Ms. Orange.

"Oh, they're having a wonderful time," said Ms. Orange. "It makes me laugh to see them trying to impress one another! Come and look!"

"You know that I'm not interested in adult-children," Mr. Orange replied.

Ms. Orange placed her adult-baby on the floor next to Mr. Orange and returned to watch the adult-children.

"What are they doing now?" said Ms. Orange to Ms. Ali.

"They are playing a game where they pretend to make the rules for the whole country," said Ms. Ali.

Ms. Orange returned to talk to Mr. Orange. "William, please come and look. The adult-children are pretending to be leaders."

"Darling," said Mr. Orange, "you know I'm not interested in such things."

Once again, Ms. Orange returned to watch the adult-children. When she entered the room, some of the adult-boys were yelling, "Yes, yes, yes!" Others were yelling, "No, no, no!" and some were simply yelling whatever they were thinking about at that time. One of the very fat and very boring adult-boys stood up and started to explain something very boring. After a very long time, he sat down. Then, another fat and boring adult-boy stood up and made another long and boring speech. Finally, one of the troublesome fat adult-boys raised his drinking glass. "To Ms. Ali!" he shouted. "Thank you for a great party." Everybody clapped.

Another adult-boy stood up and started saying something very boring, so Ms. Ali clapped her hands loudly. "Now, you've enjoyed pretending to be leaders. However, it's getting late. You can have one more dance. Then, you must all go home."

After the final dance, children came to take their adult-children home. Luckily, the fat and boring adult-boys were taken home first.

When they were all gone, Ms. Ali sat down on the sofa. "Looking after adult-children is such hard work, Ms. Orange," she said.

"They're lovely," replied Ms. Orange. "However, they really are troublesome"

Mr. and Ms. Orange put on their hats, picked up their adult-baby, and started to walk home. They passed in front of Ms. Lemon's school.

"I wonder, William, Darling," said Ms. Orange, looking up at the window. "I wonder if our lovely adult-children are asleep!"

"I really don't care what they're doing," said Mr. Orange.

"Oh, William, don't say that!"

"You think about them all the time, don't you?" said Mr. Orange.

"Yes, I do," said Ms. Orange. "I really do!"

"Well, I don't," said Mr. Orange.

"William, Darling," said Ms. Orange, pressing his arm, "I have an idea. How about asking Ms. Lemon to keep our adult-children at school during the holidays?"

"What an excellent idea! I'm sure she will be very happy to keep them if we pay her," said Mr. Orange.

"I love spending time with our adult-children, William," said Ms. Orange, "but it's probably better for them to stay with Ms. Lemon. Let's pay her to keep them throughout the holidays."

That was what made this such a nice country. Soon, all of the adult-children were sent away to school during the holidays. They were kept in school for as long as they lived, and they were made to do whatever the children told them to do.

Quiz 2.2

1. In the country where children control every-thing, what are adults called when they get very old?
2. Why did Ms. Orange decide to send all of her adult-children to school?
3. Describe Ms. Orange's visit to Ms. Lemon's house and their conversation about adult-children.
4. How did Ms. Lemon discipline the adult-children at her school?
5. Why does Ms. Orange decide to send all eight of her adult-children to Ms. Lemon's school?
6. What happened at the party for the adult-children that Ms. Ali had at her house?
7. How did Mr. and Ms. Orange's attitude towards the adult-children differ, and what idea did they eventually agree upon regarding the adult-children during the holidays?

2.3 Robin (Aged 9)

Captain Robin Braveheart is a well-known pirate. He is also the writer and hero of this story. The captain started as a pirate at nine years old. He now owns a big and strong ship called *The Beauty*. It has 100 guns.

Before becoming a pirate, the captain was an ordinary school-child. One day, however, his Latin teacher scolded him very badly for no reason. To keep his honor, the captain asked the teacher for a fight. When the teacher refused, the captain bought an old handgun, put some sandwiches in a paper bag, made a strong drink, and became a pirate.

On a lovely summer's day, the captain was sailing *The Beauty* in the South China Sea. His sailors were sitting around him. Everybody was singing.

I don't like living on land!
I feel free at sea!
Hey, hey, heave-ho!
Hey, hey, heave-ho!

Suddenly, a sailor shouted, "Whales!"

"Where are they?" yelled Captain Braveheart, jumping to his feet.

"On the front left side, Captain," replied the sailor, touching his hat to show respect. All of the sailors knew it was very important to show respect to the captain. Anybody who forgot to show respect was thrown into the sea.

"This adventure belongs to me," said Captain Braveheart, getting into a small boat.

The sailors got very excited.

"Captain's near the whales!" said an elderly sailor, watching with his telescope.

"He's caught something!" said a young sailor, pointing out to the sea.

"He's dragging it this way!" said another sailor, jumping up and down.

The captain approached *The Beauty*, dragging a whale through the water. All of the sailors yelled, "Braveheart! Braveheart!" The sailors lifted the whale onto *The Beauty*. It was very big.

"Raise the sails, Men," Captain Braveheart ordered. "We're going North West." They sailed at high speed over the deep blue sea.

Nothing special happened for two weeks. Well, nothing special for pirates happened. They captured and stole treasure from four Spanish ships and one South American ship... As I said, nothing special for pirates. The sailors were beginning to feel bored. They wanted more action and adventure.

Captain Braveheart ordered everybody to come to the middle of the ship. "Men, I hear that some of you are unhappy," he yelled. "If you want to complain about something, come forward now!"

After some time, Bill Boozy came forward. He was a very big, strong man. However, when the captain looked at him, his legs became weak.

"Speak up! What do you want to say to me?" yelled the captain, taking out his handgun.

"Well, err, well, Captain Braveheart," replied Bill Boozy, his voice shaking. "I've sailed on ships my whole life. Err, well, err, the milk in our tea on this ship is the worst I've ever ta..."

Just as Bill Boozy was saying the word "tasted," he noticed that the captain was holding his handgun. Bill stepped backward and fell into the sea. Unfortunately, he couldn't swim.

The sailors were shocked.

Captain Braveheart took off his coat and jumped into the sea. Saving such a big man was not very easy. The captain took hold of Bill Boozy's shirt and dragged him back to the ship. The sailors cheered loudly. From that day on, Bill Boozy became the captain's most trustworthy sailor.

Captain Braveheart pointed at a faraway ship. It was in a harbor. "We'll capture that ship tomorrow at dawn," he said. "Everybody can have a big glass of alcohol tonight."

In the morning, the ship, which was called *The Scorpion*, sailed out of the harbor. It fired a gun at *The Beauty*. Then, it raised a flag. It was the Latin teacher's flag.

Captain Braveheart spoke to his sailors. "Capture the Latin teacher alive," he ordered. "Now, get ready for battle, Men."

The fight began. *The Beauty* repeatedly fired its guns at *The Scorpion*. *The Scorpion* fired its guns at *The Beauty*. However, *The Beauty* was much faster and much more powerful than *The Scorpion*.

The Latin teacher was encouraging his men to fight harder. Clearly, he was a brave man. However, his clothes—his white hat, his short trousers, and his long school coat—were nothing compared to Captain Braveheart's fashionable uniform.

The two ships were side by side. Captain

Braveheart jumped onto *The Scorpion*. His sailors followed.

A fight started. When the Latin teacher saw that his men were beaten, he put down his gun and raised his hands. The captain's sailors captured the Latin teacher. They took him to *The Beauty*. Then, *The Scorpion* sank to the bottom of the sea.

The sailors gathered around the Latin teacher. The cook was particularly angry. His brother had been killed in the battle. He ran toward the Latin teacher with a cooking knife in his hand. The captain fired his handgun and killed the cook.

Captain Braveheart approached the Latin teacher. He pushed him to the ground. Then, he turned toward his sailors. "How should we punish him for scolding a schoolchild for no reason, Men?" he asked.

All the sailors yelled, "Death!"

"Yes, I agree, Men. He deserves to die," said the captain. "However, we are honorable pirates. It would be dishonorable to kill him." The captain thought for a moment. "Prepare one of the small boats!" he ordered.

A boat was immediately prepared.

"I'm not going to kill you," said the captain. "However, I will never let you scold schoolchildren again. Get in this boat. You have a compass, a bottle of alcohol, a bottle of water, a piece of pork, a bag of biscuits, and my Latin grammar book. Go to a nearby island, and live with the natives."

The unhappy Latin teacher got into the boat. He watched as *The Beauty* sailed away.

A strong wind began to blow. *The Beauty* sailed South West. Captain Braveheart was tired after the battle. He had cuts all over his body, so he went to his room to rest and recover.

The next morning, the weather turned bad. Thunder and lightning continued for six weeks. Then, hurricanes followed by tornadoes blew for two months. The oldest sailor on *The Beauty* said that it was the worst weather he'd ever seen.

Food was running out. The captain reduced everybody's food by half. Then, he reduced his own food even more. Bill Boozy noticed that the captain was eating less than everybody else was. "Captain, you need to eat," he said. "Let me kill myself. Then, you can eat my body."

"You're a good man, Bill Boozy," said the captain. "Thank you, but no thank you."

When the men were too weak to stand, a miracle happened. The sky became blue. "Land!" a sailor yelled.

"Natives!" another yelled.

Hundreds of natives were approaching *The Beauty* in canoes. They were singing loudly.

Chew-a-chew-a-chew tooth.
Munch, munch. Nice!
Chew-a-chew-a-chew tooth.
Munch, munch. Nice!

It soon became clear that the natives were planning to chew, munch and eat the sailors. The chief of the natives, who spoke excellent English, was the first to get onto *The Beauty*. He raised his arm to tell the others to attack. Then, Captain Braveheart walked toward him. When the chief saw the captain, he immediately called off the attack. He'd heard many stories about Captain Braveheart. The chief shook in fear. "Please don't kill us," he said, going down onto his hands and knees in front of the captain. The captain told the chief to stand up and promised not to hurt him.

The natives prepared a big meal for the sailors. After eating, the chief invited Captain Braveheart to his village. The captain accepted the invitation. However, he did not trust the chief, so he told his sailors to keep their guns ready.

When they arrived at the chief's village, the captain was surprised to see the Latin teacher. The natives had shaved his head, tied him to a tree, and put flour all over his body. They were planning to eat him.

Captain Braveheart spoke to his sailors. "The Latin teacher is a very bad man," he said. "However, we cannot leave an Englishman to be cooked and eaten by natives." The sailors agreed. They decided to save the Latin teacher on two conditions:

1. *He promises to never teach again; and*
2. *He spends the rest of his life doing Latin homework for schoolchildren.*

Captain Braveheart freed the Latin teacher. "Get ready for battle, Men," he said, raising his handgun. The natives started yelling when they saw that the captain had freed the Latin teacher. They angrily ran toward the sailors. "Fire your guns, Men!" ordered Captain Braveheart. "Fire! Fire! Fire!"

Hundreds of natives were killed. Hundreds were injured, and thousands ran into the forest to hide. After defeating the natives, the sailors took the Latin teacher to *The Beauty*.

This time, they sailed to a friendly island where the natives ate vegetables and pork. The chief on this island was very kind. He gave Captain Braveheart food, spices, and jewels.

When the sun came up on the third day, the captain pointed out to sea. "Raise the sails, Men!" he ordered. "We're going to England." All of the sailors cheered loudly.

After months on the open sea, *The Beauty* approached the southern coast of Spain. A ship sailed toward them. Captain Braveheart recognized its flag. It was the flag from his garden in England. It was his father's ship, *The Family*.

Bill Boozy rowed a small boat to *The Family*. When he returned, his boat was full of presents of fresh meat and vegetables. The captain's mother, father, aunts, uncles and cousins were on *The Family*. They all wanted to hug Captain Braveheart and take him home. However, the captain did not want to return home. Instead, he invited his family to a party on *The Beauty* the next day.

That night, the Latin teacher used a flashlight to send a message to *The Family*. He said that he would help them capture the captain and take him home. The sailors caught the Latin teacher. The next morning, the Latin teacher was thrown into the sea for behaving dishonestly.

The party was a great success. It started at ten in the morning and continued until seven the next morning. The captain's parents were so happy to see him that they cried tears of joy. His uncles, aunts, and cousins were amazed by the size of *The Beauty*. The captain ordered his men to fire all 100 of the ship's guns. His cousin, Tom, became excited and started to behave badly. The captain's men locked Tom in a room for a few hours to keep him quiet.

Captain Braveheart invited his mother to his private room. "Where is my bride, Alice?" he asked. His mother said that she was staying in the seaside town of Margate. However, Alice's family did not want her to marry the captain. The captain became very angry. He ran out of the room. "Raise the sails, Men," he ordered. "We're going to Margate to save Alice."

When they arrived at Margate, the captain rowed a small boat to the beach. His sailors followed. William, the captain's honorable and brave cousin, led the sailors. The captain spoke to the mayor.

"Do you know the name of my ship, Mayor?" the captain asked.

"No," said the mayor, rubbing his eyes.

"It's *The Beauty*," said the captain.

"Oh! Oh! I'm sorry," said the mayor, looking shocked. "Are you the famous Captain Braveheart?"

"I am!"

The mayor started to shake in fear. He'd heard many stories about Captain Braveheart.

"Now, Mayor," said the captain, "help me save my bride, Alice. If you don't help, I will attack Margate."

The mayor went to look for Alice. Bill Boozy went with him.

After two hours, the mayor and Bill Boozy returned. "Captain," said the mayor, "Alice is getting ready to go for a swim in the sea. When she enters the sea, I will help you to rescue her."

"Mayor," said Captain Braveheart, "you have saved your town."

The captain waited near the beach. When Alice entered the sea, the mayor rowed his boat to one side of her. The captain rowed his boat to her other side. Alice was confused. She screamed in fear. Captain Braveheart put his strong arms around Alice. He pulled her onto his boat. Alice's fear turned to joy. The captain took her to *The Beauty*.

Soon after, the mayor rang the harbor bells. It was a signal for the captain. Alice's family had agreed to let her marry the captain. A boat from the church arrived. The captain and Alice got married.

Captain Braveheart gave expensive gifts to everybody on *The Family*. They all loved the gifts. Unfortunately, the captain's cousin, Tom, became excited and started to behave badly again, so he was locked in a room to keep him quiet. However, Alice soon let him out. The sailors raised the sails on *The Beauty*. It departed for the Indian Ocean. The captain and Alice enjoyed a long and happy life together.

Quiz 2.3

1. How did Captain Robin Braveheart go from a regular schoolchild to becoming a pirate?
2. Can you share the event in the South China Sea where Captain Braveheart captured a whale?
3. Why did Bill Boozy step forward to talk to Captain Braveheart, and what happened to him afterward?
4. What caused the calm sea to turn into a severe weather situation?
5. How did Captain Braveheart deal with the Latin teacher and the locals on a nearby island?
6. What did the captain offer the Latin teacher to spare his life, and what happened when the teacher tried to betray him?
7. How did the story conclude for Captain Braveheart and Alice?

2.4 Alice (Aged 7)

Once upon a time, there was a king and a queen. The king was strong, brave, and handsome. The queen was intelligent, beautiful and kind. They had nineteen children. The eldest, Alice, was seven years old. She took care of her younger brothers and sisters.

One day, while the king was walking to his office, he stopped at the fish market. He bought some salmon and enjoyed talking to the store-owner. Then, he continued on his way. A few minutes later, a young boy came running toward him. "Excuse me, Sir!" the boy said. "There was an old woman staring at you at the fish market. Did you see her?"

The king was surprised. "What old woman?" he said. "I was the only customer."

Just then, the old woman from the fish market came running toward the king. She was wearing expensive silk, and she smelled of dried lavender.

"Are you King Rainbird?" asked the old woman.

"Yes, that's my name," replied the king.

"Is your daughter the beautiful Princess Alice?" asked the old woman.

"Yes, Alice is the eldest of my nineteen children," replied the king.

"I am a good fairy," said the old woman. "My name is Marina. When you return home for dinner this evening, politely offer Princess Alice some of the salmon you bought."

"What if she doesn't want it?" said the king.

Fairy Marina became very angry. "Don't be so greedy!" she yelled. "I know you want to eat it all by yourself."

The king lowered his head. "Please forgive me," he said.

"Be good, then," said Fairy Marina. "When Princess Alice eats the salmon, she will leave the bone on her plate. Tell her to dry it, rub it, and polish it until it shines. It's a present from me."

"Is that all?" asked the king.

"One more thing," said Fairy Marina, "the fishbone is magic. Princess Alice can use it to wish for whatever she wants. However, she can only use it once after trying very hard and after trying everything."

The king started to ask a question. "Why…"

Fairy Marina angrily kicked the ground. "Adults are *always* asking why. Why! Why! Why!" she yelled, staring at him. "Well, there is no reason!"

The king shook in fear. He promised never to ask her why again. Fairy Marina flew away, and the king continued walking to his office.

That evening, the king kindly gave Princess Alice some salmon, which she took. She enjoyed it very much. When she had finished eating, the only thing on her plate was the fishbone. The king told Princess Alice what Fairy Marina had said.

Princess Alice dried the bone, rubbed it, and polished it. It shone like a pearl.

The next morning, when the queen got out of bed, she put her hands on her head. "Oh, dear me, dear me. My head, my head, it hurts so much!" she said, falling to the ground.

Princess Alice hurried to help the queen. She

took the fishbone out of her pocket. However, when she started to wish for her mother's health, she noticed a jar of strong smelling herbs next to the bed. She carefully put the fishbone back into her pocket. Then, she held the jar under the queen's nose. The queen opened her eyes. "Don't worry, Mother. I'll look after you," Princess Alice said, pressing a wet towel on the queen's head.

The queen was very sick. Princess Alice took good care of her and all of the young princes and princesses. She dressed and undressed the baby prince. She boiled the kettle for tea, heated soup, swept the floor, and prepared the queen's medicine. She was busy from first thing in the morning to last thing at night. What's more, there were no cooks or cleaners to help because the king was too poor to employ them.

Princess Alice had a close friend, Little Lady. She told Little Lady all of her secrets. Little Lady was a good listener. To other people, Little Lady was just a doll. To Princess Alice, however, she was more than a doll. When Alice told her about the fishbone, Little Lady smiled and nodded. She only did this when she was alone with Princess Alice.

In the evenings, Princess Alice and the king took care of the queen together. The king was always angry. He wanted Alice to use her fishbone to make the queen better. Whenever the king became angry, Alice ran to her room to talk to Little Lady. "Adults think we never have a reason for doing things," she said, holding Little Lady. Little Lady smiled.

"Alice," said the king one evening.

"Yes, Father."

"Have you lost your magic fishbone?" he asked, wondering why she had not used it to heal the queen's sickness.

"No, it's in my pocket, Father!"

"Oh, I thought you'd lost it?"

"Of course not, Father."

Princess Alice took very good care of her brothers, sisters, and the queen. One day, for example, the noisy dog that lived next door tried to bite one of the young princes. As the prince ran away from the dog, he fell and cut his hand on some glass. There was so much blood. The other princes and princesses were shocked. They all started crying loudly. Princess Alice was worried that the noise would wake the queen, so she quickly put her hands over their mouths to keep them quiet. Then, she gently washed the blood from the young prince's hand and put a bandage on it.

The king quietly watched Alice. "Alice," he said.

"Yes, Father."

"What have you been doing?" he asked.

"Cleaning and bandaging, Father."

"Have you lost your magic fishbone?" he asked, wondering why she had not used it to heal the young prince's hand.

"No, it's in my pocket, Father!"

"Oh, I thought you'd lost it?"

"Of course not, Father."

After that, Princess Alice hurried to her room to talk to Little Lady. She told her what her father had said. Little Lady laughed.

Well, another time, while Princess Alice was making soup for dinner, her youngest brother, the baby prince, fell down the stairs. He injured his eye. The other young princes and princesses were shocked when they saw his eye. They all started crying loudly. Princess Alice was worried that the noise would wake the queen. She ran to the baby prince, picked him up, checked that he was okay, and gently rocked him to sleep. Next, she told the other princes and princesses to come to the kitchen. They all stopped crying and excitedly ran to the kitchen. While holding the baby prince, she taught the other princes and princesses how to make soup. They all enjoyed making soup. Then, they enjoyed eating it together.

The king quietly watched Alice. "Alice," he said.

"Yes, Father."

"What have you been doing?" he asked.

"Cooking and cleaning, Father."

"Have you lost your magic fishbone?" he asked, wondering why she had not used it to heal the baby prince's eye.

"No, it's in my pocket, Father!"

"Oh, I thought you'd lost it," he said.

"Of course not, Father."

The king sighed. He looked so sad. "Are you okay, Father?" Alice asked, putting her hand on his shoulder.

"I am so very, very poor, Alice," he said.

"How much money do you have, Father?" Princess Alice asked.

"None," he said, sighing again.

"Is there no way for you to get money, Father?"

"No," said the king, lowering his head. "I have tried very hard, and I have tried everything."

Princess Alice put her hand into her pocket. "Father, please be honest, have you really tried very hard? Have you really tried everything?" she asked.

"Yes, Alice. I have."

"Well," she said, sitting down next to him, "if you cannot succeed after trying very hard and after trying everything, you can ask for help. That's the secret of the fishbone."

Princess Alice gently kissed the fishbone. "Please make today a bonus day for my father," she said. "He has tried very hard, and he has tried everything."

Princess Alice heard a loud noise coming from the garden. Money was falling from the sky. Alice and her father ran outside. Just then, Fairy Marina came flying through the sky on a carriage pulled by four beautiful birds. She was wearing silk, and she smelled of dried lavender.

"Princess Alice," said Fairy Marina, "it's lovely to see you. Come here, and give me a hug." Alice ran up to Fairy Marina and gave her a big hug. Fairy Marina looked at the king. "How are you, King Rainbird?" she asked.

The king smiled. "I'm much better now, thank you," he said, bowing.

"Do you understand why Princess Alice did not use her fishbone to help the queen?" asked Fairy Marina. "Do you understand why Princess Alice did not use her fishbone to help the young prince and her baby brother?"

The king blushed. "Yes, now I understand," he said, nervously bowing again.

"Ah! *Now* you understand, but you didn't understand *then*, did you?" yelled Fairy Marina.

The king nervously bowed again. "No, I'm very sorry," he said, looking at Princess Alice.

"Be good, and be happy, then," said Fairy Marina.

Fairy Marina used her fan's magic. The queen and all the princes and princesses suddenly appeared. They were wearing beautiful clothes and were laughing and smiling. Next, Fairy Marina touched Princess Alice's shoulder with her fan.

Alice's old clothes changed into a beautiful silk dress and golden bows appeared on her shoes.

Fairy Marina returned to her carriage and opened the door. "After you, Princess Alice," she said. "A handsome young prince is waiting for you at the church." Princess Alice smiled. Next, Fairy Marina spoke to the king, the queen, and all of the princes and princesses. "Join us at the church in exactly 30 minutes," she said.

The carriage flew up into the sky and went to the church. A handsome young prince called Robin was sitting alone in the church garden. He was eating a sugar cube, waiting to be 90 years old.

When Prince Robin saw the carriage flying through the sky, he knew something special was about to happen. "Prince Robin," said Fairy Marina, "I have brought your bride." Prince Robin smiled. Fairy Marina touched Prince Robin's shoulder with her fan. His clothes became new. His hair became neat, and his old hat flew away.

Princess Alice and Prince Robin entered the church. Their family, friends and neighbors were waiting inside. Everybody cheered loudly.

The wedding was lovely. Afterwards, everybody

enjoyed a delicious wedding meal. The room was decorated with white ribbons and white flowers.

When the desserts were served, Fairy Marina stood up. She raised her drinking glass. "Let's drink to celebrate the marriage of a beautiful couple," she said. "I hope they have a long and happy life together." Then, Prince Robin stood up and spoke with emotion. Everybody cried tears of joy and yelled *hooray*.

Fairy Marina walked up to the king and queen. She told them that they would never be poor again. What's more, from now on, the king would receive eight bonuses a year. Then, Fairy Marina spoke to Princess Alice and Prince Robin. "Darlings, you will have 35 beautiful children, seventeen boys and eighteen girls. They will all have beautiful curly hair, and they will all be very good and healthy. They will never catch a cold or get sick."

On hearing such good news, everybody yelled *hooray* again.

"There's just one more thing to do," said Fairy Marina. She opened her fan, and the fishbone jumped out of Princess Alice's pocket. It flew through the air and landed in the mouth of the noisy dog that lived next door. From that day on, the dog was silent. It never barked at nor bit the children again.

Quiz 2.4

1. Who was the first child of the king and queen, and how old was she?
2. What instructions did Fairy Marina give to Princess Alice regarding the fishbone that the king gave her?
3. How did Princess Alice use the fishbone when the queen became sick?
4. What was the king's reaction when he found out why Princess Alice had not used the fishbone to heal the queen?
5. How did Princess Alice help when the baby prince fell and injured his eye?
6. What did Fairy Marina do to help the king and his family overcome their financial difficulties?
7. What significant change occurred when the fishbone landed in the mouth of the noisy dog that lived next door?

THE SIGNALMAN

Nouns

1. Beard: Hair that grows on the chin and cheeks of a man's face.
2. Compartment: One of the sections into which the interior of a vehicle or structure is divided.
3. Disaster: A sudden event, such as an accident or a natural catastrophe, that causes great damage or loss of life.
4. Duty: A moral or legal obligation; a responsibility.
5. Eyebrows: The strips of hair growing on the ridge above a person's eye sockets.

6. Forehead: The part of the face above the eyebrows.
7. Handkerchief: A square piece of cloth used for wiping the eyes or nose or as an accessory in one's attire.
8. Path: A track or way made for walking.
9. Post: A vertical support or structure, like a light post, to which something, such as a sign or light, may be attached.
10. Signal-box: A building from which railway signals are controlled.
11. Signalman: A person employed to manage the signals and switches on a railway.
12. Torment: Severe physical or mental suffering.
13. Tunnel: An underground passage through which trains travel.

Verbs

1. Emphasize: To give special importance or prominence to (something) in speaking or writing.
2. Stare: Fix one's gaze on someone or something for a long time.
3. Shake: To move back and forth or up and down with rapid, forceful, jerky movements.
4. Tuck: To put something into a small, confined space.
5. Zigzag: To move from left to right in a zigzag pattern or course.

Adjectives

1. Damp: Slightly wet, often in a way that is unpleasant.
2. Firm: Having a solid element.
3. Ghostly: Of or resembling a ghost, especially in being very pale or translucent.
4. Pale: Light in color or having little color.
5. Scared: Frightened; feeling fear.

Adverbs

1. Carefully: In a way that deliberately avoids harm or errors; cautiously.
2. Hesitantly: With hesitation; in a tentative or unsure manner.
3. Patiently: Calmly and without complaint.

HOLIDAY ROMANCE

Nouns

1. Adult: A person who has reached full physical maturity, typically classified as being 18 years old or older.
2. Alcohol: A liquid substance that can intoxicate when consumed and is often used for recreational or medicinal purposes.
3. Armchair: A comfortable chair with side supports for the arms, typically used in bedrooms or living rooms for relaxation.
4. Biscuits: Small baked bread products that are typically crisp and flat, often enjoyed as a snack or with tea or coffee.
5. Bone: The hard tissue forming the skeleton of vertebrates, providing structural support and protection for the body.
6. Bonus: An extra payment or reward given in addition to what is expected or usual,

typically provided as an incentive or recognition of good work.

7. Captain: The person in charge of a ship, aircraft, team, or group, responsible for leading and overseeing operations.

8. Captive: A person or animal that is confined or held prisoner, often against their will.

9. Carriage: A vehicle with four wheels drawn by horses or often powered by machinery, used for transportation or as a ceremonial conveyance.

10. Cherry: A small, round fruit with a seed or pit in the center, typically bright red when ripe and often used in desserts or eaten fresh.

11. Cleaner: A person or device that cleans or removes dirt and impurities from an object, surface, or environment.

12. Compass: An instrument used for navigation that shows direction relative to the cardinal directions (north, south, east, west).

13. Cornet: A brass instrument similar to a trumpet but shorter and wider in shape, often used in marching bands or orchestras.

14. Court: A place where legal proceedings take

place, or the residence of a monarch, or an area designated for playing certain sports.

15. Coward: A person who lacks courage in facing danger or difficulty, often characterized by a tendency to avoid confrontation or risk.

16. Dessert: A sweet course served at the end of a meal, typically consisting of fruits, pastries, cakes, or other confections.

17. Doll: A lifelike or decorative toy or figurine, often in the form of a human or animal.

18. Emperor: A male monarch who rules an empire, typically an emperor holds supreme authority and may be considered as the sovereign ruler.

19. Fairy: A mythical being or spirit often depicted as a delicate, supernatural creature with magical powers.

20. Fan: A device consisting of a series of vanes or blades that can be rotated to produce a current of air or cooling effect.

21. Fees: Payments made for services rendered or certain privileges granted, often associated with professional services or membership.

22. Firework: An explosive device used for

entertainment or celebration, typically pro-
ducing colorful or luminous effects when
ignited.

23. Flashlight: A portable electric light source
typically powered by batteries and used for
illumination in dark or low-light conditions.

24. Ground: The solid surface of the earth, particularly as a place for walking or building
structures.

25. Handgun: A firearm designed to be held and
fired with one hand, typically smaller than a
rifle or shotgun.

26. Harp: A large, stringed musical instrument
with a triangular frame that is played by
plucking the strings with the fingers.

27. Holiday: A day set aside for celebration,
remembrance, or rest and recreation, often
marked by special events or observances.

28. Hurricane: A severe tropical cyclone with
strong winds exceeding 74 miles per hour
(119 km/h), often accompanied by heavy
rains and storm surges.

29. Joy: A feeling of great pleasure and happiness,

often associated with success, good fortune, or fulfillment.

30. King: A male monarch or ruler of a kingdom, holding the highest authority within a country or territory.

31. Latin: A classical language of ancient Rome and the ecclesiastical language of the Roman Catholic Church, known for its literature and historical significance.

32. Magic: The practice of using supernatural forces to influence events, often associated with spells, illusions, and mysterious powers.

33. Marriage: The legally or formally recognized union of two people as partners in a personal relationship, often symbolizing a lifelong commitment.

34. Natives: Indigenous or original inhabitants of a place, often referring to the first people who lived in a particular region.

35. Pirate: A person who engages in acts of robbery or criminal activity at sea, typically involving theft of cargo or attacking ships.

36. Pond: A small body of standing water, typically shallow and surrounded by land, often

naturally formed or created for decorative or recreational purposes.

37. President: The elected head of a republic, typically serving as the highest-ranking official of a country.

38. Queen: A female monarch or ruler of a kingdom, often holding a position of authority equal to a king.

39. Rug: A floor covering made of thick woven material or animal skin, often used to cover floors for warmth or decoration.

40. Scorpion: A predatory arachnid with a curved tail containing a venomous stinger, often known for its threatening appearance.

41. Silk: A fine, soft, and shiny fabric produced by silkworms, often used for clothing or textile products.

42. Streetlight: A tall outdoor light fixture mounted on a pole beside a road or path, providing illumination for pedestrians and vehicles.

43. Tear: A drop of saline fluid produced by the eye, typically triggered by strong emotions, irritation, or injury.

44. Telescope: An optical instrument used for viewing distant objects, typically with magnification capabilities for astronomical or terrestrial observation.

45. Thunder: The loud rumbling or crashing sound produced by the rapid expansion of air heated by lightning, often accompanied by flashes of light during a thunderstorm.

46. Tornado: A violent windstorm characterized by a twisting, funnel-shaped cloud extending from a thunderstorm to the ground.

47. Treasure: Valuable items or wealth often hidden or kept in a secret location, typically associated with riches, gold, or jewels.

48. Trial: A formal examination of evidence before a judge or jury to determine guilt or innocence, often part of legal proceedings.

49. Umbrella: A handheld device consisting of a collapsible canopy attached to a central pole, used for protection against rain or sunlight.

50. Uniform: A particular set of clothing worn by members of an organization, group, or profession to indicate unity and identity.

51. Vacancies: Unoccupied positions or rooms

that are available or waiting to be filled, often referring to job openings or available spaces.

52. Whale: A large marine mammal with a streamlined body and a blowhole for breathing, often found in oceans and known for their massive size.

53. Willow: A type of tree or shrub with narrow, long leaves and flexible branches often found near water, typically known for their graceful appearance.

54. Wine: An alcoholic beverage made from fermented grapes or other fruits, often enjoyed for its rich flavors and varieties.

55. Witness: A person who has seen or observed an event, typically providing testimony or evidence based on their firsthand knowledge.

Verbs

1. Agree: to have the same opinion or be in harmony or conformity.
2. Approach: to come near.
3. Arrive: to reach a destination.
4. Attack: take hostile action against someone.
5. Behave: to act or conduct oneself in a specified way.
6. Boil: to bring a liquid to the temperature at which it bubbles and turns to vapor.
7. Celebrate: to acknowledge a significant event with enjoyable activity.
8. Cheer: to shout in praise or support.
9. Consult: to seek information or advice from.
10. Continue: to persist in an activity or process.
11. Cry: to shed tears, typically as an expression of distress, pain, or sorrow.
12. Decline: to refuse politely.
13. Deny: to state that something is not true or happening.
14. Dress: to put on.

15. Fall: to move downward, typically rapidly and freely without control.
16. Guide: to show or indicate the way.
17. Hug: to hold someone closely in one's arms.
18. Interrupt: to stop the continuous progress of an action.
19. Knock: to strike a surface with a hard blow.
20. Plan: decide on and arrange in advance.
21. Position: to place someone or something in a particular position.
22. Pretend: to behave as if something is the case when it is not.
23. Scold: to criticize or reprimand someone angrily.
24. Sigh: to emit a long, deep audible breath expressing sadness, relief, tiredness, or a similar feeling.
25. Succeed: to achieve the desired aim or result.
26. Trip: to stumble or lose balance.
27. Wait: to stay where one is or delay action until a particular time.
28. Witness: to see something happen.

Adjectives

1. Angry: Feeling or showing strong displeasure or hostility.
2. Beautiful: Pleasing the senses or having qualities that give pleasure.
3. Boring: Not interesting or dull.
4. Brave: Showing courage or willingness to face danger.
5. Curly: Having curls or spiral locks.
6. Dishonorable: Not bringing or deserving honor.
7. Expensive: Costing a lot of money or valuable such as silk.
8. Fashionable: Conforming to the current style or trend.
9. Handsome: Attractive in a striking way.
10. Honorable: Being honest, fair, or worthy of respect.
11. Intelligent: Demonstrating good mental capacity or sharpness.

12. Intelligent: Having good understanding or high mental capacity.
13. Neat: Orderly, clean, or tidy.
14. Stubborn: Refusing to change one's mind or course of action.
15. Troublesome: Causing problems or difficulty.

Adverbs

1. Carefully: With close attention and caution, taking care to avoid mistakes or harm.
2. Gently: In a mild, tender, or delicate way, being soft or gradual in action.
3. Kindly: In a kind or pleasant manner, showing goodwill or compassion.
4. Nervously: In an anxious or uneasy manner, showing signs of tension or apprehension.

THE SIGNALMAN

The Mysterious Signalman

1. The signalman initially did not notice the narrator as he was staring into the tunnel, but he acknowledged the narrator's presence upon the second call.
2. The signalman's workplace was described as lonely, sad, wet, lacking sunlight, and had a strange smell with cold winds blowing along the tracks.
3. The signalman's tasks involved monitoring the red light at the tunnel entrance, showing flags to trains, talking to drivers, and

remaining close enough to the signal-box to hear the bell ring.

4. The signalman shared that he used his time alone to learn a new language (mostly reading), and to study fractions, decimals, algebra, and science when he was younger but struggled with numbers.

5. The signalman seemed to feel lonely, lost in thought, serious, and somewhat fearful or preoccupied during the conversation with the narrator.

6. The signalman suggested the narrator return for another visit at ten o'clock the following night and advised the narrator not to call out when finding the way up or returning down.

Visions and Warning Signals

1. The narrator returned to speak to the signalman the following night at eleven o'clock.

2. The signalman behaved politely and allowed the narrator inside the office where they sat down by the fire.

3. The signalman explained that he mistook the narrator for someone who had been causing trouble, waving and shouting near the red light in the tunnel.

4. The signalman described how he heard someone shouting "Hello, below!" followed by a bad accident on the tracks and a subsequent death.

5. The signalman felt troubled by the recurring appearances of the mysterious man, his warning signals, and the resulting accidents, causing him to feel anxious and unsure about preventing further disasters.

6. The narrator notice that the bell did not ring when the ghostly man rang it.

7. The signalman was worried about sending warnings of danger to train drivers as he feared they would think he was insane, potentially putting his job at risk.

A Chilling Revelation

1. The narrator decided to encourage the signalman to see a doctor the next evening.
2. The narrator saw a man standing next to the red light, covering his face with his left arm and waving his right arm.
3. The signalman was killed that morning after being hit by a train.
4. The train driver, Tom, explained that as he turned the corner in the tunnel, he saw the signalman at the end and did not have time to slow down before the train hit him.
5. The warning shouted by the train driver as he approached the signalman was, "Hello, below! Look out! Look out!"
6. The narrator noted that the warning from the train driver included not only the signalman's troubled words but also the narrator's phrase that the signalman had mimicked.
7. Despite the train driver's efforts to alert the signalman by shouting and waving his arms,

the signalman was hit by the train as it came out of the tunnel, resulting in his tragic death.

HOLIDAY ROMANCE

William (Aged 8)

1. William is in charge of writing all four stories.
2. William and Nettie first met at dance school.
3. Robin lit a firework to celebrate William's marriage.
4. The initial plan to rescue Nettie and Alice involved using fireworks, but it had to be changed due to cost.
5. Nettie's note implied that she thought William was too scared to attack Drowvey and Grimmer, calling him a "coward."
6. The trial ended before a judgment could be passed, but William was cheered for following orders during the attack.
7. The group pretended to be older by acting like they were 90 years old while sharing cherries under the willow tree.

Nettie (Aged 6.5)

1. In the country where children control every-thing, adults are called adult-babies when they get very old.
2. Ms. Orange decided to send her adult-children to school because they were causing too many problems.
3. During her visit to Ms. Lemon's house, Ms. Orange inquired about the availability of vacancies for adult-children at the school and discussed the school's fee, food quality, and discipline methods.
4. Ms. Lemon disciplined the adult-children by making them stand in a corner, tapping them gently for misbehavior, and directing them to exercise or improve their behavior as needed.
5. Ms. Orange decided to send all eight of her adult-children to Ms. Lemon's school

because they were becoming too hard to control.

6. At the party, some adult-children behaved badly, while others refused to dance.

7. Mr. Orange showed little interest in adult-children, while Ms. Orange was more involved in their activities. They agreed to pay Ms. Lemon to keep the adult-children at school during the holidays to maintain discipline and structure.

Robin (Aged 9)

1. Captain Robin Braveheart became a pirate after a disagreement with his Latin teacher, which led him to challenge the teacher and become a pirate at a young age.

2. Captain Braveheart caught a whale in the South China Sea, creating excitement among his sailors.

3. Bill Boozy complained about the low-quality

milk on the ship and accidentally fell overboard, but the captain rescued him and earned his trust.

4. The calm sea turned into a stormy and challenging period with thunderstorms and food shortages, which Captain Braveheart managed by reducing food rations for everyone, including himself.

5. The captain dealt with the Latin teacher by sparing his life but banishing him to a nearby island, where he negotiated with hostile natives to ensure the safety of his crew and the teacher.

6. The Latin teacher's betrayal led to his demise, as he was caught and thrown into the sea after trying to harm the crew.

7. The story ended with Captain Braveheart and Alice getting married after a daring rescue, leading to a joyous and adventurous journey together in the Indian Ocean.

Alice (Aged 7)

1. The eldest child of the king and queen was Princess Alice, who was seven years old.
2. Fairy Marina instructed Princess Alice to dry, rub, and polish the salmon bone till it shines, as it contained magic powers for making wishes.
3. Princess Alice thought about using the fishbone to help her mother. However, she put it away when she saw some herbs that could help.
4. The king understood Princess Alice's actions after he realized she used the fishbone wisely in other situations.
5. When the baby prince injured his eye, Princess Alice comforted him and showed the other children how to make soup.
6. Fairy Marina magically solved the king's financial troubles by showering the garden with money and providing bonuses for him regularly.

7. Finally, the magic fishbone was used to silence the noisy dog, making quiet by landing in its mouth.

Matatabi Press is always looking for new talent. If you fall into any of the following categories, please contact us at press@matatabi-japan.com:

- A writer interested in sharing your story with the world
- An EFL/ESL professional passionate about creating English graded readers
- A Japanese language specialist looking to collaborate on a Japanese graded reader
- A Japanese-English translator eager to translate Japanese literature

We encourage you to get in touch with us and become a part of our team.

Sentence Complexity

Matatabi Readers are categorized by sentence complexity and headword count.

Sentence Complexity	Flesch-Kincaid Grade
400	1 to 2
500	2 to 3
600	3 to 4
700	4 to 5
800	5 to 6
900	6 to 7
1000	7 to 8
1100	8 to 9
1200	9 to 10
1300+	10+

The Flesch-Kincaid Grade Level Formula is used to calculate sentence complexity. Grade Level "3 to 4" (Level 600), for instance, indicates that the sentence complexity is suitable for third- and/or fourth-grade students in the U.S.

Headword Level and Count

Headword Level	Headword Count
D	301 to 400
E	401 to 500
F	501 to 600
G	601 to 700
H	701 to 800
I	801 to 900
J	901 to 1000
K	1001 to 1100
L+	1101+

Headword Count in a Matatabi Reader indicates the number of words with distinct meanings.

Each word is counted only once, regardless of the number of times it appears in the book. This applies to verbs, adjectives, and nouns, including all their forms. For example:

- "Eat," "ate," "eaten," and "eating" count as one headword.
- "Tall," "taller," and "tallest" count as one headword.
- "Cake" and "cakes" count as one headword.

Josh MacKinnon (Adaptor)

Josh MacKinnon is an experienced Japanese-English translator, checker and proofreader. He is based in the UK and specializes in website and advertising material translation.

John McLean (Series Editor)

John is an associate professor at Yasuda Women's University in Hiroshima, Japan, where he oversees the Department of English Interpreting Stream. He is known for his Japanese translation and interpreting skills, which he has demonstrated in his work with prominent figures in the media, athletics, film, and entertainment industry.